Selkie Skin

Risa Fey

Selkie Skin

Risa Fey

Selkie Skin
Copyright © 2015 by Risa Fey
All rights reserved.

This is a work of fiction, inspired by true events. Names, characters,
businesses, places, events, locales, and incidents are either the products of
the author's imagination or used in a fictitious manner.

Paperback First Edition: 2018
ISBN: 9781720238713

For Information and Contact:
risa@risafey.com
www.risafey.com
Twitter: @Risa_Fey
Facebook.com/RisaFey

Claim your FREE stories when you join the TOP HAT TENTACLE SOCIETY today!

Top Hat Tentacle Society

Visit risafey.com

GASKON FISHER AND HIS three sons heaved the net onto the deck. Hundreds of silver fish spilled onto the plank boards, hopping and flapping in futility. Tangles of seaweed bestrewed the net here and there, along with a couple of baby dolphins that had been scooped up during the midwater trawl. Sea birds hovered, swooped, and scavenged for free meals, knocking beaks at one another while the fisherman's sons set to sorting and icing the piles of cod and haddock.

Sean, the eldest, hesitated at a boulder-like creature that was writhing underneath a heap of smaller game. The great mound was mottled with black and brown, and gleamed with the sheen of brine. It shifted and lurched, rocking back and forth, its tail cloven into two rudimentary hind-flippers.

"Father," he said, "a seal."

Gaskon rushed forward and turned the creature over by yanking its taloned flipper.

Its eyes went wide and drooped with fear. The whiskers pulsed rhythmically as it leered in frozen terror at its captors.

Appraising the creature, Gaskon rubbed a hand

through his grizzled beard, then said to the three boys, "Put it in one of the cages."

"But all the cages are too small," said Ronan, the youngest.

"It doesn't matter," said the fisherman. "If you can't fit it in, you'll just have to make it. There's a market for these."

"But it's still alive," Ronan persisted, "uninjured, even. We could set it free."

"I'll not have you question me in the face of a direct order." Gaskon glared at the impudent boy, who frowned but reluctantly gave in to the injunction.

The three sons lured the confused animal into a rusty steel-barred cage. When the seal was secured they returned to sorting through the day's catch, while the motor glided the boat gently back inland.

Sean hung back by the cage for a few minutes, having seen the seal's form distort and deflate, like a rippling amoeba. The furred flesh slipped away like a duvet, and a woman sat upright from underneath it, her fire red hair draggled into rat's tails, her trembling lips blue with cold rime. She blinked bright celadon eyes at him, and winced into the heatless evening.

Sean thought immediately of the sirens; but then he realized just as quickly that she must be what was known to sailors as the selkie, a sea-born shapeshifter that was far tamer than the deadly siren.

If he recalled the legend correctly, then any selkie

whose pelt was stolen by a man was bound in matrimony to him for as long as he retained it.

And that gave him an idea. Tolerable women in their tumbledown village were scarce, and he decided resolutely it would behoove him to take the selkie's pelt for himself.

Sean waited until she had removed her legs and feet from the sealskin. Then he snatched at it; but she recoiled like a whip, gripping the sodden hide to her chest. He yanked at a corner of the pelt, but she snapped it vigorously out of his hand and out of reach.

Angry now, Sean rounded to the other side of the cage where she was squashed up against the bars, and took the skin within his grip. He pulled with such strength that he very nearly overpowered her, but desperation gave improbable strength to her supple fingers, and she clung onto the pelt as if for dear life.

Casting a glance over his shoulder, the selkie emitted a burring sound, as if in appeal for someone's aid.

Curious as to which of his brothers she was soliciting, Sean turned, only to have the selkie's nails pierce the rough flesh of his hands like tiny daggers.

Hollering, he let the sealskin go.

"What's going on?" grated the familiar voice of his father. The gruff man froze midstride. "What's a woman doing in the cage?" But then he eyed the pelt she was desperately clinging onto. "It can't be," Gaskon said hesitantly, "a selkie maiden?"

Sean frowned, tending to the bloodied scratches on his knuckles. "What do you say we do with it?" He raised his head with the question. "Still insist on the black-market? She'd bring in a fortune."

The old fisherman waved the suggestion off and then stepped closer to the cage.

"What then? Selling her would make us filthy rich; we could give up all this hard labor."

"Some things are worth more than monetary profit." The old man grinned nastily through yellowed teeth.

Sean gazed at him in weary understanding, recognizing in his father the same hunger that was in himself.

Gaskon unsheathed a dagger and opened the cage, demanding the defenseless maiden to surrender the pelt. "Give it!" he roared. "Give it now, or I'll skin your human hide right here and now!"

Frightened at the shaking of the blade, the selkie threw it at him and backed fearfully away against the furthest bars. Salty tears streamed down her pallid cheeks as she watched him take the magick garment in his greedy fingers.

Gaskon crumpled the sealskin into a burlap bag, relocked the cage, and left the selkie with a triumphant sneer.

Sean raced after his father, pleading for the sealskin—for Gaskon to appoint her as his wife. "Please, Father," he said, "you know I haven't been able to find a wife. If you don't want to sell her then give her to me, that way I can carry on our family's name."

Gaskon's mouth tightened into a grim line. Greediness glinted in his eye. "You may be my eldest, but you're still young enough to have your pick of all the wenches in the village. I, on the other hand... I'm an old widower, and have little chance for remarriage..."

"Unfair!" Sean exploded.

"Living alone isn't good for an old man."

"But you've already had a family, and I haven't." There was unmistakable resentment in his tone.

"You'll heed and respect my wishes," said his father. "If I want her for myself, then I will have her. Now... get back to work. Go help your brothers."

Gaskon ordered his secondborn to fetch a clean outfit for the selkie. Finbar blinked, and turned to look at the naked girl. "Gods." He dropped the haddock in his hands and ran to the cabin to retrieve some clothes, which he offered the caged woman through the bars.

Finbar trained one anxious eye upon her, and then both. Her cool hands closed around the ratty garments, and her sea-green eyes flitted in examination of his features. And then he left the selkie alone, his heart lurching into such spasms of elation that he had never felt before in all his twenty years of life.

After she covered herself in the oversized shirt and trousers, Gaskon returned and reopened the cage to allow her to roam free on the gut-strewn deck. She padded about on her little fairy feet, inspecting every weatherworn crate and wooden barrel, touching paint-chipped exteriors, feeling out the strange textures of dry objects. With one hand steadied on the gunwale, she gazed out at the glittering sea, feeling much like a goldfish trapped in a small glass bowl. The magickal compulsion to remain onboard—for her sealskin was in the fisherman's possession—kept her decidedly in place. Kept her amenable. Kept her yoked to Gaskon as an involuntary wife.

After rolling into harbor and unloading the sorted crates for market, Gaskon shooed his three dazzlestruck sons away from the selkie before leading her off to her new home. When inside, he transferred the sealskin from the bag to a padlocked chest.

The selkie settled on a wooden chair in the far corner. She scanned the unclean surroundings: surfaces filmed with dust and freckled with green colonies of mold.

Gaskon commanded her to prepare their supper.

Unresponsive, she merely stared at him.

The back of his hand cracked across her delicate nose, sending her careening out of the chair and against the armoire.

"Get to it!" he barked furiously. "And don't you dare provoke me again."

Dutifully, she rushed to do as he had asked. Snatching up spoons and pots, she arranged them on the stove, like a woman long familiarized with the kitchenry of Men.

Belatedly, and as if it were an afterthought, Gaskon asked, "What is your name?"

Crockery clanked, and the selkie strained to hold back an upsurge of tears. She disregarded the question, and instead distracted herself with searching the cupboards for dry ingredients.

"Woman!"

She said nothing.

Gaskon hovered near, making the light wisps on the back of her nape stand uncomfortably on end. He glided his grubby fingers down the length of her long body, eyeing the men's apparel on her small and fettered frame. He very gently touched her cheek—but then shoved her face with enough force of violence that she reeled aside and lost her footing.

"Hurry it up," he said. "I'm starved."

Her hands shook unsteadily over the unwarmed stovetop, and a bright hot wave of fear swelled through her body.

That night, Gaskon ate and drank. When his belly was full, he jabbed a thumb to the bedroom cot. Unwilling, the selkie sat still in her place.

Furious at her hesitance, Gaskon stood up.

* * *

A BELT OF STARS dappled the black sky overhead. The

night was bracing, filled with the phantom echoes of predatory howls and nocturnal song. Sean arrived late that evening, with a leather pouch containing some instruments and devices that his father had left behind on the trawler ship.

As he approached the stony doorstep, he heard a raucous shouting and a high squealing coming from indoors. He rushed to the nearest window, heard a successive pounding of fist flesh upon flesh—and through the splintered slats of the louvers, Sean spied his father in the act of battering the selkie bride, evidently priming her for a rape.

Or so it appeared. Indeed, he was tearing at her clothes. Gaskon trussed her wrists against the small of her back and jostled her head down, smothering her face into the bed sheets, all while tugging at her jean trousers.

Without a moment's delay, Sean threw the front door open and took the nearest heavy object—a ceramic urn filled with his mother's ashes—and struck his father in the back of the head with it. Incapacitated, Gaskon fell onto the half-naked selkie. Sean threw him off onto the floor, kicking him in the stomach for good measure.

Sweeping the trembling selkie up in his arms, Sean fled the house and stole her away to his own home.

Laying her on top of his cot, Sean gathered a washbasin and clean cloth, and patted her bruises and wounds with the wrung wet linen. After soothing the selkie out of her panic, he very gently kissed her on the forehead and then smiled warmly.

Sean sat on the bed, wrapped an arm around her, and buried his lips into the tangled web of her red hair. In the quiet that followed, he listened to the soft rumor of vibration in her throat: either a lingering groan of fear, or a tame soft purring.

He eventually removed himself from holding her, and the frightened selkie watched him through sad eyes as he donned a jacket and then left on his horse for the village market. Just as the emporium was locking its doors, he managed to buy a proper woman's outfit. He also stopped in time at the medical shop to pick up some utensils and solutions to treat her wounds with—although he dreaded how she would react to the cold of metal and the sting of tincture.

Returning home, he was surprised to find the selkie cooking at his stovetop in the nude. Stumbling over himself at the unexpected sight, he straightened up again and brushed the clinging dust off from his knees.

She turned and smiled by way of greeting, looking every bit the contented wife, he thought.

Sean closed the door and made his slow way toward the decrepit table, on which he set the bag of goods.

"I'm sorry for what I said before—talking like you were an animal," he uttered low. Unable to refrain himself, he raised his curious eyes and stared at the fiery cloak of hair veiling her perfect figure from his view. "May I ask your name?"

She placed the wooden spoon down and glanced inquisitively at the bag set on the table.

"Just some clothes," he answered, "and some first-aid I thought you might need." Sean's eyes, almost of their own volition, explored the half-turned profile of her body, and his heart skipped with the beginnings of impure longing. He tore his gaze away with a mighty conscious effort, before saying: "What if I just called you Meara? It seems to suit."

"Sean." Her whisper was so quiet that he could have believed the voice was inside his head. "I like 'Meara' just fine." She returned to her stirring, and his heart clenched within his chest.

"What are you making?" he asked. "I've already had supper."

"It's not for tonight," she said. "Whiskey tablets for tomorrow."

His face broke out into a smile. "I haven't had those in years."

She smiled sidelong at him, teasingly, and he couldn't help but turn slightly red.

"Put these clothes on," he said, and then he removed himself to another room, feeling suddenly inspired to give her some privacy. Meara poured the syrupy mixture into a metal tray for it to cool, and then she busied herself with browsing through the bag.

But as she slid the rose-gold gown over her head, a

scalding sensation lashed over her lower back like a bolt of lightning. Her screaming was so dreadful that Sean flew back into the kitchen in a wild panic.

"What is it?" He took hold of her by the shoulders, but that only seemed to make her cry the more. Meara clawed and tore at her flesh, as if at an unseen infestation, and she writhed in his arms before folding forward with a shriek.

At first, Sean was too stunned to think what to do; but then a patch of her skin bubbled and burst before his very eyes, peeling away like a desiccated curl of burning paper. A mottle of charred skin bloomed over the apple of her cheek, and tiny whorls of smoke uncoiled from the blackened surface, carrying with it the unbearable stench of burning flesh.

Horrified, he staggered backward, but eventually the rational part of his mind took over.

Sean left Meara in the house, and he ran across the desolate landscape—knowing his horse would be no good on the off-road rocky terrain. He passed a line of slumbering cottages before coming upon his father's home. Gaskon's cottage was the only one in the vicinity with a yellow glow still flickering in its windows—and he knew, with darkening fury, what that meant he would likely find.

Confirming his worst expectations, Sean went in and found his father singeing portions of the sealskin. He sprung at the old man, but his father bulldozed him with a hefty butting of the shoulder.

"So!" Blood trickled from the head wound, down the side of Gaskon's face. "It was *you*."

Sean spat. "You're mad if you think scarring her will bring her back!"

"I own the sealskin, you petty thief," Gaskon said, and his breath came ragged. "She is already all mine, and you cannot have her."

"Well *I* think destroying the very magick that makes her yours is all the same as forfeiting her love."

The old man shook the sealskin within his grasp. "*My* bride. I will do with her what I damn well please."

In the next moment, father and son locked arms, and they threw each other about the room, vying for dominance. After several minutes of breathless scuffling, Sean shoved his father a bit too forcefully, and Gaskon stumbled back onto the burning gas lamp on the bedside table.

Glass shattered. Oil spattered. A raging fire bloomed. Flames caught onto Gaskon's clothes, enwrapping his limbs like tenacious snakes.

The sealskin fell from the old man's grasp and lingered dangerously close to the brink of the spreading fire. Sean plucked it up, and beat off the wayward embers from its fibers.

Meanwhile, not five feet away, Gaskon flailed and hollered from within the unquenchable pickets of flame. Shadows shivered about the room as the flames grew large and hissed and sputtered. Flammable objects were pelted by specks of ember, and the walls ignited. The curtains roared, and the wooden foundations were blanketed by a bed of ravenous flames.

Sean faltered, turned about, and ran.

The heat of the fire lingered on his face, even as he raced through the bitter cold. Chill winds nipped at his cheeks and burned his nose, and the sealskin smoked and streaked the air with the remnants of an ashen haze.

In minutes he was home, incoherent and raving about his father's death. Rage peppered his cheeks in the form of tears, and the selkie dabbed them with the hem of her new gown. She cradled his head to her blistered bosom, but the pungency of burnt skin reminded him to tend to her scattered wounds.

There was no need for Meara to fully disrobe, but he pressed poultices and salves against the lesions, dressing them loosely with tape and gauze. "My father," Sean said, breaking the heavy silence, "drove my mother to suicide with the way he treated her." He used his teeth to cut a new bandage, and then continued on: "Their marriage was the stuff of nightmares, but she never bore up the courage to leave him. Now he's dead..." And he seemed to be taking a moment to digest that. "I only hope to never be like him."

* * *

FINBAR, THE MID-SON, visited Sean's house around noontime the next day. He hadn't expected the selkie bride to be there, but the surprise was pleasant, if not dubious. Hiking his feet up on the table, he indulged his curiosity by asking Meara about the sea and her arcane heritage. She was discouraged by the subject, since it evoked a melancholy longing for the sea that she knew might never be satisfied.

After noticing the discolored patches on her cheek, Finbar asked, "Did you burn yourself this morning?"

"Yes," she lied. "My hand slipped, and the pan splashed oil on me." She shrugged self-consciously. "Now I know to pay better attention while I'm cooking."

Finbar's eyes lingered at her swanlike neck. "Since I was a boy," he said, "Mother told us about the legend of the selkie. We knew it was a true story, especially since there was a man at a neighboring village who had had his children by one." She met his eye, and he could sense he now held her full attention. "Seven years and three surviving children later, the selkie found where he'd been hiding her magick skin. The poor man never saw his bride again."

Meara could not help but ask: "What happened to the children?"

"They never saw her again either." He leaned further back and folded his arms.

"You were my father's just the other night," Finbar pursued when they were alone. "So how did you become my elder brother's...?"

"Your father gave him my sealskin," Meara answered, purposefully omitting the whole truth.

He raised his brows. "And so it's true: whoever owns your skin is the husband you must cling to. You have... *no* say in the matter, whatsoever?"

Her dignity dampened, she bore her chin up. "That is correct."

Sean came and went as they discussed the matter further, listening in on the conversation with ongoing unease. As he glanced at his new bride, she met his eye in such a way that, despite her not saying so, Sean knew he could trust her to keep mum about the previous night's incident.

Finbar's eye strayed to the rocking chair, located opposite him below the window. Straining within his seat, his knuckles grew white. Draped across the chair-backing was the maculated sealskin, rumpled and foolishly forgotten by its owner.

His attention returned to Meara, but she was busy about her work, bustling to a fro. It occurred to him that she was probably waiting for him to leave so she could retrieve the skin and flee. But it *also* occurred to him that now was his chance to gain the perfect wife without the courtship and the hassle.

Meara placed and replaced the same empty vessels; moved and removed the same utensils. Finbar noted the growing anxiety in her movements, the wearying impatience, and the oversweet indifference to his conversation.

When Sean returned again, wiping his hand off with a rag, he and Meara exchanged glances, and this time her eyes were pleading.

Sean rounded the table and sat across from his younger brother. Throwing the rag down on his lap, he pulled out a short paring knife, reached for an apple nestled in the bowl set on the table, and started cutting at its flesh. He snapped a crisp white piece off, tossed it in his mouth, and chewed. With a profound expression of boredom, Sean said, "What are you bothering my wife about?"

"Nothing at all." Finbar detected the implied threat in Sean's handling of the knife. "We were only talking about her kind."

"And what, pray tell, makes you think she wants to discuss *that*?" The brutal glitter in Sean's eyes dared his younger brother to press further. "She no longer lives in the sea. She lives *here*. She's not an animal anymore, she is a woman. She is *my* wife—my property, and not the Sea's."

"But she came from—"

"She could come from the stars for all I care." Sean cut the apple clean in half, then stuck the blade tip into the tabletop before standing up. "I think you have somewhere else to be."

"Sean—"

He cut him off. "And take your damned feet off the table, you bloody cad."

Meara watched Finbar from the corner of her eye as he promptly took his feet down.

"Alright," he said, "But you could use some help carrying in the rest of the wood from the barn. You've got a lot of work later on, and a man ought have a little bit of time to spend with his new wife. Let me help while you go off and be with her, and then I'll leave."

Sean could think of no reason to refuse the generous offer, and so he shrugged. "I'd appreciate it. But don't speak to her from now on, do you understand?"

Finbar nodded, and immediately went about his new employment: carrying the wood in at a slow pace, and in smaller quantities than was necessary. Meara was running out of credible occupations to bide her time with, and her husband—who was now watching her from the table with the apple halves in hand—now seemed dubious of her directionless activity.

"He'll leave you alone," Sean said when Finbar was out of earshot. "You can stop wracking your nerves now."

At once she stopped, feeling overcome by a wave of nauseating homesickness.

His teeth snapped pieces from the apple halves, and his eyes became heavy with longing as he traced her figure with an idle gaze.

All of a sudden, he wanted Finbar gone. But no, he

said to himself. It wasn't quite time for that. The day's tasks had to be seen to, and soon Meara would be preparing them their first shared lunch. In time, they would come together, and the ritual of procreation would come naturally. Sean got up from the chair and slipped an arm around the small part of her waist.

Meara leaned against his side. The sweat of labor was slick on his skin, and the smoke of cigarettes clung to his clothes. "Come along," he said. "If he bothers you that much—" Finbar was just crossing by the breakfast nook when he overheard "—then I'll distract you outside." He kissed her hair and jutted his nose into the sea-smell of her curls.

"But I still have so much to do," Meara said automatically, and with instantaneous regret.

"You've done nothing but move around in circles."

Finbar lowered a heap of wood into the backroom, and listened carefully as Sean said: "Come on. Let's go. Don't quarrel. We'll find something to do."

The sound of shoes scraped along the floorboards, signaling a leisurely departure. When the wooden creaks and groans had stopped, Finbar hurried from the backroom. He plucked up the sealskin, checked their location beyond the window, and left out the backdoor in blind haste.

* * *

NIGHTFALL CHASED THE warm sun into hiding. A delicate knocking rapped at Finbar's door. He opened it, finding the selkie maiden in her nightgown on his doorstep. With a gracious sweep of the arm, he welcomed her inside. "Good evening."

Meara's neck was rigid, and she said nothing.

"You'll be happy here," he reassured.

She shot him a glare.

Meanwhile, Sean was retiring from his fieldwork. He called for Meara as he went indoors, his belly aching and limbs sore. A minute passed, during which she did not respond.

He sat at the table and placed a hand over his bloodshot eyes. "Meara," he called again, before whispering more softly, "damn it, woman..."

Again, no response. Not even the busied shuffling of skirts.

The unnatural silence roused him back onto his feet. Sean walked to each of the sparse rooms, expecting on each entry to find her reclined lazily over a chair or in a bed. But he never found her. When he went to the backroom and saw that there wasn't nearly enough wood piled up from the storage barn, he froze, panic seeping slowly into his blood. He went over the same rooms again, this time grazing their contents more thoroughly with his eyes.

Meara was nowhere to be found.

Hanging his head outdoors, he called her name, ran a

circuit around the house and—seeing nothing—rushed back inside in a red-eyed rage. It was then that Sean finally noticed the uncovered rocking chair under the window. The sealskin wrap was gone.

Sean took to the road on horseback, with only a knitted scarf to keep him warm. Upon arriving at his younger brother's house, he pounded a fist into the wood of the front door. "Give her back!" he roared, and then began charging the door with his full bodyweight.

The door busted open on the fourth charge, and he collared his brother and threw him to the ground, off the bed and away from his stolen bride. He boxed Finbar in the ears, jarring the man long enough to land another three blows to the stomach. "You thieving pus," he cried, "I'll crack your skull in."

Taking advantage of the skirmish, Meara hopped to her feet and scuttled toward the sealskin, which was lying on a dilapidated crate. But Sean snatched up the sealskin first—his younger brother grabbing at it second.

They struggled to overpower one another, punching and kicking, tugging and tearing, unwilling to relinquish the key to her matrimonial enslavement.

Unsheathing the paring knife from his belt, Sean made as if to attack his brother. But Finbar raised the sealskin up on impulse, using it for a shield, and the steel edge sailed down in a silver arc. The knife slashed the bulk like butter, leaving a long cleft down the center of the pelt as Finbar attempted to wriggle free.

Meara keened and cried. But neither of the brothers stopped even as they heard her wailing.

Finbar caught his brother's wrist just as the knife was being jabbed at him once again. He planted a knee into the vulnerable region of Sean's gut, wrenched the knife from his grip, then stuck it hilt deep into his chest.

Sean grew still as the sharp penetration shocked him into docility. Heat gushed from the wound, flooding down the brown front of his shirt, a black-red murk.

Finbar stumbled against the wall. Numb with a strange mixture of relief and guilt, he grit his teeth and watched as his brother drowned in lungfuls of his own blood.

Sean crumpled to his knees, and then very gradually groped his way down onto the floor.

Meara convulsed. Her skin—now notched with various cuts—trembled and quaked. The throb in her ears grew to a crescendo, and she opened her mouth to speak, wanting nothing now but to be back in the protective womb of the sea.

"I want to go home," she said, and the words repeated into a chant. "Please... *please*, let me go home..."

Ignoring her, Finbar left the house with the mangled sealskin in his hand. Upon entering the stable adjacent to the cabin, he whipped open a heavy blanket from among a crateful of extra blankets, and refolded it with the sealskin tucked away inside its folds.

Returning to the cabin, he gathered alcohol and swabs and stitching needles. But before settling down to patch Meara up, he wrapped the corpse of his brother in burlap and dragged it out through the front door. Heaving the corpse onto the back of Sean's horse, he led the packing animal by the reins and disposed of the body in the ebbing tide of the sea.

Black water lapped around the unwieldy bag and dragged it further out from land. Foam whipped over the bopping top before it sank.

* * *

TWO DAYS PASSED. The hapless bride was going about the marketplace, procuring food while covered from head to toe in a dress meant to conceal her scars. She hobbled along like a cripple, her legs slashed, and gouged thighs chaffing beneath the pleats. But her gait did not go unnoticed by the youngest of the Fisher brothers, Ronan.

Jumping down from a potato cart, Ronan moved in on the wandering selkie, slowing down to keep stride with her. "Hello, Meara." He had heard her give that name to one of the vendors.

Meara avoided being reeled into a conversation, but Ronan straggled along awkwardly at her heels, not wanting to let go of his chance to talk to her.

"You look like you're in pain," he said more boldly, and she stopped to root around a colorfully laden vegetable cart.

Hefting a head of cabbage up, the lace of her sleeve fell back, revealing a bracelet of dried scars. Ronan stepped closer on a sympathetic instinct—but then retreated. Gazing at her profile, he was better able to see the disfigurements she failed to conceal beneath her bonnet and scarf.

After she paid for the cabbage, he said, "I hope you don't think I'm being too intrusive, but, Meara, you look like you've been beaten."

She paused and stared into his blue eyes.

"Would you at least give me the pleasure of helping you out?" Ronan extended a chivalrous hand toward the basket hanging on her arm.

Astonished by the gentle offer, she passed him the basket without a word, and he laid it over his own arm. "I have more shopping to do," she said shyly, picking at her fingernails and glancing around them apprehensively.

His lips drew back into a grin. "Very well. I've nothing but time to kill here anyway."

Ronan tagged along like a hardy mule, strapping bags crosswise over his body, and strategically rearranging the sacks of flour and white sugar from hand to hand. Honestly, he couldn't imagine how she would've managed without his help; but then again, it was entirely possible she was only taking advantage of the opportunity.

Women were sly that way sometimes.

Meara hugged a bag of flour to her chest, since Ronan had no more muscle to spare. As she turned to him, he asked directly, "If I unload these for you at your home, will you tell me how you got those scars?"

Only after a brief hesitation, they set the sacks and packages down on the ground, and Meara confessed to him the whole truth: about Gaskon's death, and his older brothers' fatal dispute.

"They fought each other to the death for you...?" His tone was almost disbelieving.

She nodded, feeling more horrible than flattered over the situation.

Ronan reflected for a while. "It's the sealskin, isn't it? That's what binds you, like a wedding band, to your mate."

"Yes," she said.

"How come?"

Meara shrugged. "It's just the way things are."

"Well then." He paused, feeling more uncomfortable the more he thought about it. "I'm sorry." He came closer, staring slantwise at her face.

"I'm the one who should be sorry," Meara replied. "Your father and brother are dead because of me."

"It's tragic," he agreed. "But they only did it to themselves..."

Her chin went down.

"I suppose Finbar will pretend he doesn't know what happened to Sean. And you—" His voice shook slightly as he looked at her. "For what it's worth, I'm sorry for what they did to you."

She smiled sadly. "It's no use feeling sorry for what can't be changed." And then in an effort to change the subject: "Anyways, I'm done here. We should leave."

"Where did you hitch the horse?"

Meara's smile disappeared. "I wasn't allowed to take one, I'm afraid."

Ronan frowned, wondering what made his brother do something so unreasonable.

Together they hitched a ride on a wagon. Finbar was not at home by the time they arrived, and so Ronan stayed to help Meara unpack. Taking a bag of flour from her arms, he surprised her by stealing a kiss all in the same gesture. He smiled in a way meant to convey affection, but the selkie shunted around him.

"You don't have my skin," she reminded him, her tone firm and clipped.

"Maybe not. But neither did Sean—" and he caught himself, thinking better of his words. After a speedy recalculation, he went on to say: "I seriously doubt you're in love with my brother. If given a choice, you'd prefer to be back in the sea—away from him."

Her face nearly tightened into a scowl.

"Why don't you *ignore* who has your skin?" he said.

"Go back to your home, or come live with me instead."

"I can't." She clutched a bag set on the table. "If I do, I'll have broken myself. There's nothing I can do to change it."

"But you don't belong here."

"He'll burn me out from hiding—just like your father tried to do."

"Any man who would do such a thing is not in love."

"Exactly." Her mouth trembled on that point, and she leveled her gaze on him.

Ronan sighed in apparent defeat.

"None of them loved me," she went on. "They each wanted something else—not someone to love..."

Ronan placed the bag of flour down, looked around the space of Finbar's cabin. "Where's your sealskin?"

Tears welled within her eyes. "He hid it from me after he killed Sean."

He cast his eyes down.

"You should probably leave now," Meara said, getting fidgety. "He'll be back soon, and he'll be wondering why you're here."

"It's getting cold out." Ronan started for the door.

"Let me get you something, then." She abandoned her chore and crossed the yard to the barn where she knew some extra materials were stored. She dug out a blanket that looked serviceable enough, and handed it to Ronan after going back in the house. "There you are. He won't miss that one."

His doting eyes met hers.

Meara dug her chin in, her cheeks becoming inexplicably hot.

Ronan started home, turning again and again to gaze back at the shackled bride, his glances amorous and smile contrite.

Meara closed the door just as he was opening up the blanket.

Velvety fur grazed his thumbs, a texture inconsistent with the woolen blanket-weave. Ronan recognized what it was immediately. But rather than return the sealskin to her, he continued on, wrapping both layers around his shoulders, keeping the tattered animal pelt cloaked stealthily underneath. A smile spread across his face.

* * *

MEARA PLACED A COUPLE of plates on the table, and ladled portions of food from three steaming pots. She and Finbar ate in silence. He didn't complain about the food, but he was agitated over the speed of her quick eating. Placing his fork down, he said, "I can't help but get the feeling you can't wait to get away from me."

Meara froze, the spoon poised readily at her lips. "I'm tired is all." But, heedful of his keen awareness, she slowed herself down.

When they had finished, she washed the pots and ceramic plates in the basin under the water pump. After storing away leftovers in the icebox, she untied the pristine apron from around her waist and shoulders, and then hung it on the hook.

That was when it happened. A prickling sensation traveled down the side of her flank.

Meara struck a hand over the area and rubbed, baffled when the feeling failed to disappear. Instead, it spread down the curve of her waist, moving halfway down her outer thigh. It felt like a suture needle, a tightening of threads, as if her flesh was a garment being crimped and stitched together.

Trying her best to ignore it, she went to the bedroom where Finbar was changing into his nightwear. The prickling continued still, the needle-fine punctures getting more numerous.

Meara left the room in a mild panic. Whirling into the kitchen, she peeked under her clothes where the cause of the painful itching could be seen. Tiny lines of angry red were seamed along the upper portion of her breast. Small pinpricks of irritation formed a smooth and patterned line.

Heart thundering in her chest, she paced the compact room, wondering how she was going to hide them from her husband when she *knew* he would be expecting to make love. She was no longer beautiful and immaculate, she thought. Covered head to toe in blemishes and blotches, she felt the worth and worthiness of her beauty stretching thin and wearing down.

Finbar emerged and noticed the look of quiet panic on her face. "Something the matter?"

"No." Meara spun around, trying to get a grip over herself.

But she had responded too quickly. Distress was evident in her voice.

"Something's wrong," he said, stepping around so that he could face her. It was a declaration, not a question. "Tell me what."

But she refrained, gradually regaining mastery over herself. "I promise you, it's nothing."

"Are you nervous of sharing with me tonight?" he asked, turning her chin up with his hand. "I know you must still be hurting from everything that's happened, but I promise to be gentle."

"I'm still in pain from the *inside*," Meara emphasized with earnest, and she saw that that would be enough to keep him off. As impatient as Finbar was, it was obvious he still cared at least a little. "Please, can we wait a little longer...?"

"I don't *want* to wait."

"And you also don't know what Sean did to me when he cut my sealskin." She was growing in confidence now, watching as his anger gave way to grudging sympathy. "If you do any more damage on top of that—"

"Very well."

Dropping his hands, Finbar started toward the bedroom alone.

The stippled heat stitching her skin gradually abated from her breast. By the time her husband was asleep, Meara slipped noiselessly onto her own side of the small bed. And then unexpectedly, she felt a watery coolness lapping at her flesh.

Although she wasn't in any water, it gave her the impression of being so. The smell of sea salt was on the air, and imaginary waves enveloped her all around. Her sealskin, she realized with delight, must be somewhere along the shore!

Meara glided out of bed and stole barefoot out of the house. She ran across the gray cragged landscape, to the nearby waves and foaming sea. Her gown billowed like a trail of smoke in her wake, and her heart quickened as she impelled herself to greater speed.

A dark figure stood silhouetted against the moonbright waves, heavily cloaked, a piece of fatty garment whipping through the wind in his strong grip. As she came near, she recognized him, and he held the mended sealskin out for her to take.

Tears spilled from Meara's eyes. "How did you...?"

"You gave it to me." Eager, Ronan started to approach. "It was buried in the blanket that you gave me. You must not have known..."

Tramping through the sand, her hand touched the familiar fur. But she stopped herself from taking it. "Aren't you going to claim me also?"

Ronan opened the sea-soaked pelt, and wrapped it

around her little shoulders like a cloak. He drew her in by its collar. "Is that the only way I can have you?"

"He'll come for you," she said. "He'll fight, even if you don't."

"Then go," he said. "I can't force you to stay. But if you're safe—that's all I want."

Meara blinked, feeling his words like a flutter of butterflies in her chest. She scrunched her brow. "If I go home, I can never come back to either of you."

Ronan smiled in sad acknowledgment. "I know the legend."

Chagrined, she staggered back as he released the enchanted pelt, restoring it to her charge.

A shout from behind Meara broke their shared silence. Finbar was flailing from afar, tripping over rocks and reeling his arms, the bright glint of a knife cutting through the air.

Meara's hand went instinctively for the hunting knife at Ronan's hip. Wedging the blade so that it nicked the border of her sealskin, she dragged the sharp steel down its entire length, paring the thick pelt clean in half. She convulsed in a blind agony of pain as the laceration sliced over her own body. The pelt's twain pieces hung limp in her hand, and blood flooded in rivulets down the front of her gown, seeping into the pearly sand at Meara's feet.

Horrified, Ronan caught the wilting selkie in his arms, but she regained herself enough to stand, supported by the buttress of his strong shoulders. She wrapped one of the skins over his back like a mantle, tugging it tight around his neck. He shook with shock, gazing into the fainting light of her celadon eyes. Against his pleas, she put the other remaining half around herself, then squeezed him tight within her arms.

"Take me to the sea," she said in a level voice, and he gaped at her in a powerless confusion.

Finbar rampaged down the sand like a crack of thunder, and Ronan guided the limping selkie into the agitated waves. The rising water lapped around their calves, and Meara threw him—and then herself—into the sea.

Finbar dove after them in a rage, feeling wronged and betrayed to the point of murder. But the water beneath the surface was black as ink, and his human eyes couldn't penetrate the cloud of lightless murk. Losing his way, he became disoriented, not knowing which way was up or down. Believing he was fighting towards the moonlit crests, he chased after a rogue gleam of phosphorescent light. But when the luminous object came within his view, he realized all too late it was a bottom-feeding invertebrate signaling for its prey.

Water filled his lungs. Finbar's vision closed in, smearing out the remaining light. Death stole him away, and his body gave up the futile struggle. His vacant corpse hovered in a peaceful grave, claimed by the Sea, where his flesh would be eaten, his white bones stripped and infiltrated to the marrow.

Ronan's lungs contracted painfully as the water pressed in all around him. Something was propelling them like a motor through the water, but he could not imagine what.

Believing he was at the end of his life, he took one final gasp—and then snapped his eyes open as he realized at that moment he could breathe.

The force propelling them downward was the rudder of Meara's tail, the swishing lunges of her swollen body. No longer a woman—and he no longer a man—they dove and swirled into the freezing depths where the water's pressure would be too great for any human to sustain.

The selkie's laceration leaked a red trail through the brine. Meara slowed, tired and feeble from the injury. Ronan nudged her worriedly with his newly whiskered nose, but her responses faded out.

The sea was a black maze to him, and he did not know what to do or which way to go. To regain the shore was just as impossible as finding help in the barren void. Disheartened, the male selkie opened his mouth to mourn and groan.

Eventually they both came to a complete stop.

Ronan wrapped his neck around hers, patting a desperate flipper against her flank. Unmoving, Meara simply drifted with the slow sway of the currents.

Plankton sprung up all around them, dim glows of microscopic phosphorescence. With his groaning ceased, Ronan settled against the warmth of his dying mate.

A muffled swishing vibrated curiously at his ears. A swarm of seals broke out from the unseen groves below, and they whirled in astonishment at the stranded, wounded pair. With bays of recognition, they nose-butted the couple down, and further down—to where the kelp forests grew out of rock grooves, and the seaweed rippled like dense ribbons.

The pod of seals wrapped Meara in makeshift bandages of kelp strips, and laid her to rest in a protective hollow of coral-studded rock. They dispersed and captured tiny stray fish in their teeth, delivering them to her anemic mouth, and they clicked at her to fight for strength and chew for nourishment.

Meara closed her eyes, stealing a woozy nibble here and there.

Ronan spun about and looked down curiously at his tail—at the diminutive feet-like flippers. He bayed happily before reclining against his bride.

The End

Claim your FREE stories when you join the TOP HAT TENTACLE SOCIETY today!

Top Hat
Tentacle Society

Visit risafcy.com

Support readers and INDIE creators by leaving an honest review.

~

<u>MORE BOOKS BY RISA</u>

risafey.com
Or:
amazon.com/author/risafey

Made in the USA
Las Vegas, NV
27 January 2025

17115092R00025